Tractor Mac
YOU'RE A WINNER

Tractor Mac

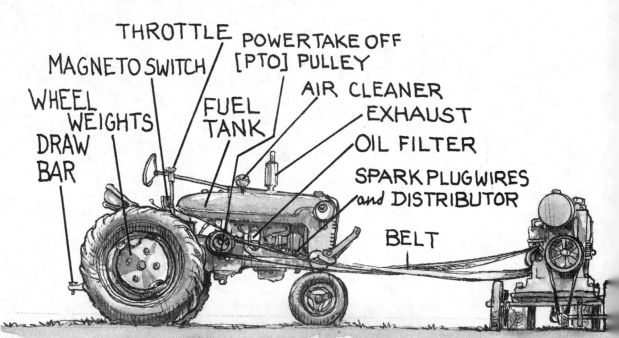

THROTTLE

MAGNETO SWITCH

POWER TAKE OFF [PTO] PULLEY

WHEEL WEIGHTS

FUEL TANK

AIR CLEANER

EXHAUST

DRAW BAR

OIL FILTER

SPARK PLUG WIRES and DISTRIBUTOR

BELT

Carousel

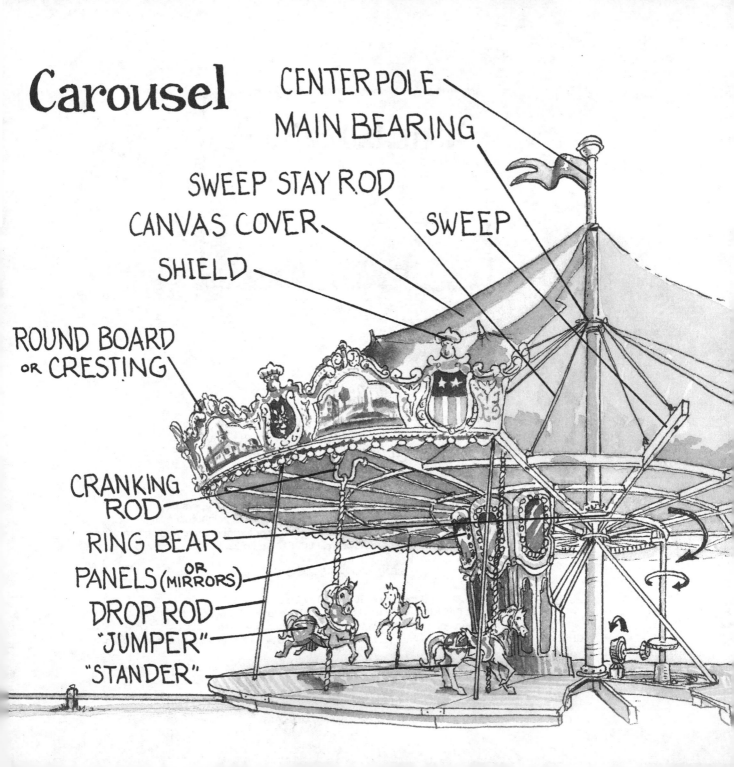

CENTERPOLE

MAIN BEARING

SWEEP STAY ROD

CANVAS COVER

SWEEP

SHIELD

ROUND BOARD
OR CRESTING

CRANKING
ROD

RING BEAR

PANELS (OR MIRRORS)

DROP ROD

"JUMPER"

"STANDER"

This Is MyBook

_____

For my sons,
Trip, Wil & Nate
Blue Ribbon Winners each!

ISBN 978-0-545-53793-3

12 11 10 9 8 7 6 5 4 3 2 1   13 14 15 16 17 18/0

Printed in the U.S.A.   40

First Scholastic printing, May 2013

Tractor Mac
YOU'RE A WINNER
written and illustrated by Billy Steers

SCHOLASTIC INC.

The big event was almost here! For months, Tractor Mac and Farmer Bill had been getting ready for the big tractor pull contest at the county fair.

"I can remember all the great horse pulls at the fair," said Sibley the workhorse.

"I'm sure I can pull the weights the farthest and win that contest!" said Mac. He felt as strong as ten tractors.

"I hope you win, Mac!" said Tucker Pickup.

"WOOF YIP!" barked Fetch the dog.

Finally the day of the big pull came. "Good luck!" bellowed Margot the cow as Tucker pulled Mac to the fair.

The fairgrounds were full
of things to see and do. There were
rides and a brightly painted carousel.
Music played and children laughed. "This
will be a happy day!" thought Tractor Mac.

The pulling arena was crowded with many tractors
from all over. Big blue ones. Huge orange ones.
Giant green ones.

Tractor Mac suddenly felt very small.

The announcer called
the tractors to the ring
one at a time.

Mac did great in his first round. He pulled the heavy blocks easily. The Line Judge shouted, "FULL PULL!" when Tractor Mac had reached the end of the track.

"The day's not over yet," said a big tractor named Deke. "Only the *really* strong tractors make it to the finals."

The tractors had to work harder as the loads got heavier. By midday, more than half of the tractors were out of the event. They couldn't pull the weights far enough.

By late afternoon, only two tractors were left: Tractor Mac and Deke.

"Don't *hurt* yourself, Mac," laughed Deke after he pulled the biggest load yet.

It was Mac's turn again.
This was it!
"Do your best!" said a little bulldozer nearby.

Heave! *Tug!* **PULL!**

Mac pulled as hard as he could. The load inched forward, Mac's engine roared, and his tires bit into the sand. Finally, he could pull no farther. The crowd waited to hear the judge's call.

Mac had been beaten!

Deke had pulled the same weight, but pulled it one foot farther.
Mac felt like crying as he watched Deke collect first prize.

Slowly, Tractor Mac left the arena and
passed through the fairground on his way out.
The carousel stood still and quiet. Fair workers were trying
to fix the broken generator. Children sadly watched and
waited. What an unhappy day this was.

Suddenly, Farmer Bill had an idea! He parked close and hooked Mac's power belt to the carousel.

Mac throttled up, the belt spun, and music played!
The colorful animals came to life, and laughing
children climbed back on board!
  "Hooray for the big red tractor!" everyone shouted.

For the rest of the day, Mac helped run the carousel. When it was time to go back home, he could hardly wait to tell everything to his friends at the farm. Farmer Bill smiled proudly and said, "Tractor Mac, you're a *true* winner!"

Billy Steers is an author, illustrator, and pilot. In addition to the Tractor Mac series, he has worked on forty other children's books. Mr. Steers had horses and sheep on the farm where he grew up in Roxbury, Connecticut. Married with three sons, he still lives in Roxbury.

Tractor Mac

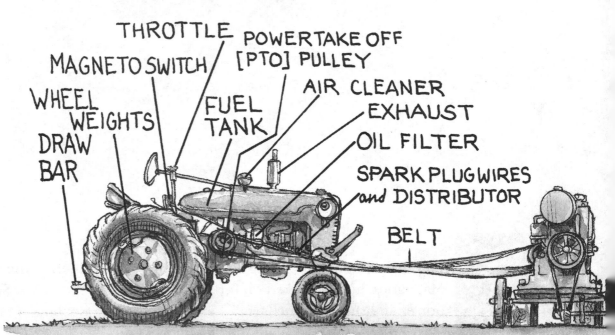

THROTTLE

MAGNETO SWITCH

POWER TAKE OFF
[PTO] PULLEY

AIR CLEANER

EXHAUST

WHEEL
WEIGHTS

FUEL
TANK

OIL FILTER

DRAW
BAR

SPARK PLUG WIRES
and DISTRIBUTOR

BELT

Carousel

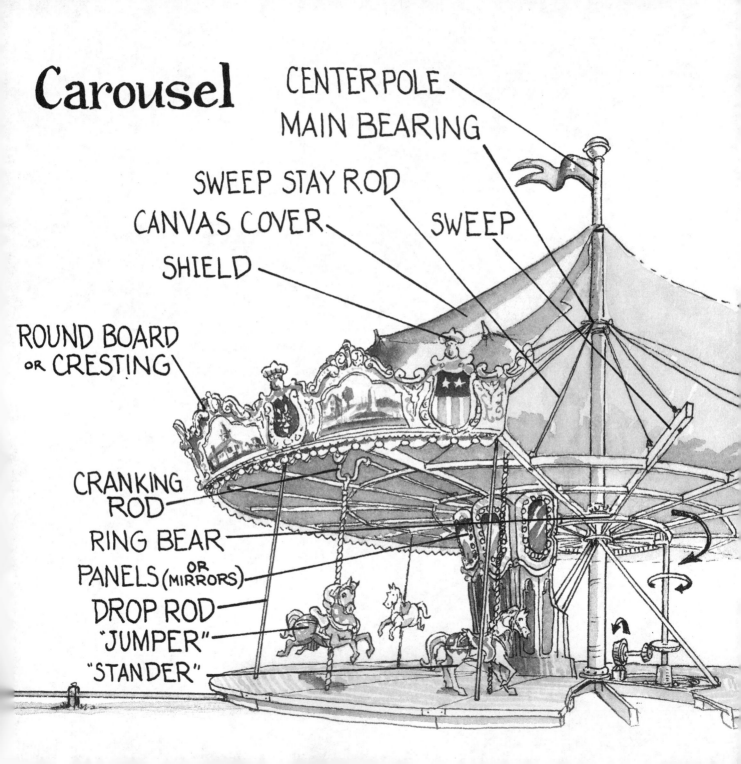

CENTER POLE

MAIN BEARING

SWEEP STAY ROD

CANVAS COVER

SHIELD

SWEEP

ROUND BOARD
or CRESTING

CRANKING
ROD

RING BEAR

PANELS (or MIRRORS)

DROP ROD

"JUMPER"

"STANDER"